DATE DUE

Welcome to
Hopscotch Hill School!
In Miss Sparks's class,
you will make friends
with children just like you.
They love school,
and they love to learn!
Keep an eye out for Razzi,
the class pet rabbit.
He may be anywhere!
See if you can spot him
as you read the story.

# Welcome!

Miss Sparks

Delaney

Hallie

Logan

Gwen

Avery

Spencer

Nathan

Razzi

Skylar

Lindy

Connor

Published by Pleasant Company Publications
Copyright © 2005 by American Girl, LLC
For information, address:
Book Editor, American Girl, 8400 Fairway Place,
P.O. Box 620998, Middleton, WI 53562.

Visit our Web site at **americangirl.com**.

Printed in China
05 06 07 08 09 10 C&C 10 9 8 7 6 5 4 3 2 1

Hopscotch Hill School™ and logo,
Where a love for learning grows™, Delaney™, and
American Girl® are trademarks of American Girl, LLC.

Cataloging-in-Publication data available from the Library of Congress

# The One and Only Delaney

by Valerie Tripp illustrated by Joy Allen

# Merrily, Merrily, Merrily, Merrily

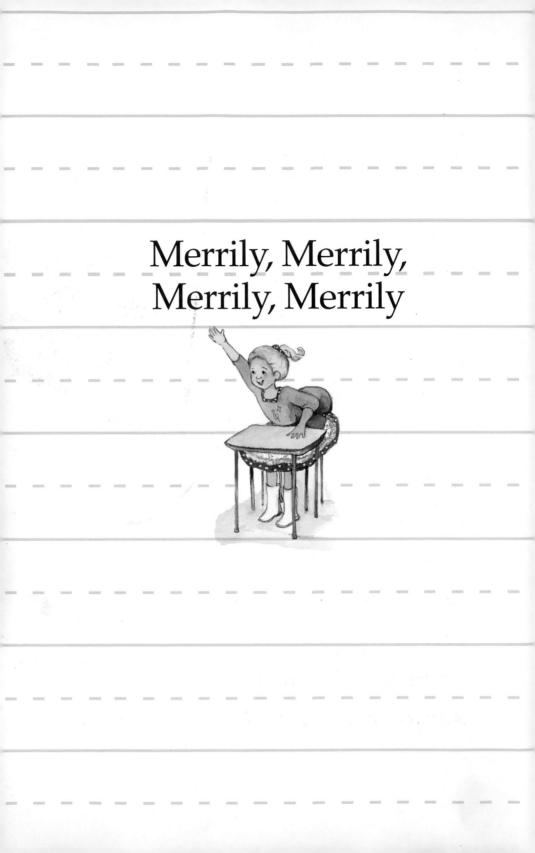

One morning Miss Sparks said,
"Oh, Delaney! I like your skirt!
Please tell us about it."
Delaney skipped
to the front of the room.
She twirled around.
All the children said, "Oooh!"
Delaney said,
"I love this skirt
because it has
musical notes on it.
And I love music
because it makes people happy."
Logan said, "We know
that you love music, Delaney."

"Yes!" said Skylar.

"You are always humming

or whistling or singing."

All the children said,

"That's right!"

Miss Sparks sat down

at the piano and asked Delaney,

"What is your favorite song?"

Delaney said, "'Row, Row,

Row Your Boat.'"

Miss Sparks said, "Let's sing it now!"

All the children sang,

"Row, row, row your boat

gently down the stream.

Merrily, merrily, merrily, merrily,

life is but a dream."

Spencer pretended

that he was rowing a boat.

Soon all the children were rowing!

When the song was over,

all the children

clapped and smiled.

9

The sparkles on Miss Sparks's

eyeglasses glittered.

She said, "Delaney is right.

Music can make people happy!

Can't it, children?"

All the children said, "Yes!"

Then Miss Sparks said,

"Let's pretend that we have

rowed our boats

all the way to the sea.

What creatures live in the sea?"

Lots of children raised their hands.

The class was learning about

fish, crabs, seabirds,

sea horses, snails, whales, and all sorts

of creatures that live in the sea.

Avery raised her hand and said,

"We might see whales."

Miss Sparks said, "Yes!"

She pointed to

three pictures of whales.

She said, "We might see these

three whales."

"Oooh," said all the children.

Miss Sparks asked,

"Who can use the words

**big, bigger,** and **biggest**

to tell me about these whales?"

Connor raised his hand and said,

"The gray whale is big.

The black whale is bigger.

The blue whale is the biggest of all."

"Yes!" said Miss Sparks.

"**Big, bigger,** and **biggest**

are words we use

to compare things."

Miss Sparks held up

three pictures of fish.

She said,

"We might also see these

three fish in the sea.

Who can use the words

**small, smaller,** and **smallest**

to compare these fish?"

Gwen raised her hand and said,

"The green fish is small.

The purple fish is smaller.

The red fish is the smallest of all."

"Yes!" said Miss Sparks.

"**Small, smaller,** and **smallest** are

words we use to compare things."

Lindy said, "I like sea creatures."

All the children said, "Me, too!"

Miss Sparks smiled.

She said, "In two weeks our class

is going to give a program for

other students here at

Hopscotch Hill School.

Would you like our program

to be about sea creatures?"

All the children said, "Yes!"

Miss Sparks said, "Splendid!

You may each choose

a sea creature.

I will help you decide

how you want

to share information

about your sea creature.

You can draw the sea creature.

You can talk about it

or write a poem about it.

You can pretend

to be the sea creature.

You can work on your

presentations by yourself

or you can work with friends."

Delaney said, "I'd like to do

a presentation about whales!

Who wants to work with me?"

Avery said, "I do!"

Skylar said, "Me, too!"

Delaney said, "Great!

It will be fun to work together."

Miss Sparks smiled.

# The One and Only Delaney

Miss Sparks said, "Children,

do you know that some whales

hum or whistle or sing?

Who does that remind you of?"

All the children called out, "Delaney!"

Miss Sparks said, "That's right!

Let's sing Delaney's

favorite song again."

Everyone sang,

"Row, row, row your boat

gently down the stream."

Miss Sparks sang loud.

The children sang louder.

And Delaney sang the loudest of all,

"Merrily, merrily, merrily, merrily,

life is but a dream."

# Good, Better, and Best

Delaney, Skylar, and Avery
were very excited
about their whale presentation.
Skylar found three books
about whales.
Skylar said, "Let's read these books
to find out more about whales."

Delaney and Avery said, "Okay!"

The three girls began to read.

At first Delaney hummed happily.

But then she stopped humming.

Her book was hard to read!

Delaney looked at Skylar.

Skylar was not having any trouble

at all reading her book.

Delaney said, "Hey, Skylar!

My book is too hard for me.

May I read your book instead?"

Skylar said, "Sure!"

Skylar and Delaney traded books.

Again Delaney tried to read.

But Skylar's book was harder

than the first book.

Delaney looked at Avery's book.

Delaney saw that Avery's book

was the hardest book of all!

Delaney did not know what to do.

She had always thought

that she was a good reader.

But now she compared herself

to Avery and Skylar.

Delaney could see that Skylar was a
better reader than she was.

And Avery was the best reader of all.

Delaney said sadly,

"I am not very good at reading.

I think I should choose something

else for my presentation."

Avery and Skylar looked sad.

Slowly they said, "Well, okay."

Just then Hallie said, "Oh, Delaney!

Please come work with Lindy and me.

We are drawing pictures of seabirds."

"Okay!" said Delaney. "I like seabirds!

I will draw a seagull."

At first Delaney whistled happily.

But then she stopped whistling.

Her drawing did not look pretty.

Delaney looked at Lindy's drawing.

Lindy's drawing of a

duck was much prettier than

Delaney's drawing of a seagull.

Then Delaney looked at

Hallie's drawing.

Hallie's drawing of a pelican

was the prettiest drawing of all.

Delaney did not know what to do.

She had always thought

that she was good at drawing.

But now she compared herself

to Lindy and Hallie.

Delaney could see that

Lindy was better at drawing

than she was.

And Hallie was the best of all.

Delaney said sadly,

"I am not very good at drawing.

I think I should

choose something else

for my presentation."

Lindy and Hallie looked sad.

Slowly they said, "Well, okay."

Just then Connor said, "Hey, Delaney!

Come work with Gwen and me.

We are going to show how crabs walk.

Watch!"

Connor and Gwen

put their hands on the floor.

Lickety-split, quickety-quick,

they walked sideways like crabs.

Delaney said, "That looks like fun!"

Delaney put her hands on the floor.

Lickety-split, quickety-quick,

Delaney walked sideways like a crab.

At first Delaney sang

happily to herself.

But then she

stopped singing.

She was too out of breath to sing!

She could not

walk sideways very fast.

Delaney looked at Connor.

Connor could walk sideways

much faster than she could.

Then Delaney looked at Gwen.

Gwen could walk sideways

the fastest of all.

Delaney did not know what to do.

She had always thought

that she could move fast.

But now she compared herself

to Connor and Gwen.

Delaney could see that

Connor could move faster

than she could.

And Gwen could move

the fastest of all.

Delaney said sadly, "I am not

very good at walking like a crab.

I think I should choose

something else for my presentation."

Connor and Gwen looked sad.

Slowly they said, "Well, okay."

Then Logan said, "Howdy, Delaney!
Come work with Spencer
and Nathan and me.
I am writing funny
poems about sea horses.
Nathan is writing funny
riddles about snails.
Spencer is writing
funny jokes about fish.
Would you like to write
something funny too?"
Delaney shook her head sadly.
She said, "No thank you."
Delaney was discouraged.
She knew that Logan was funny.
Nathan was funnier.

And Spencer was the funniest of all.

When Delaney compared

herself to them,

she didn't feel very funny at all.

Delaney sighed.

She sat down by herself

next to the piano.

Miss Sparks came by.

Miss Sparks said, "Hello, Delaney!

I am making a list of presentations.

What will you be doing

for our program?"

Delaney looked down

at her hands in her lap.

"Nothing,"

she said softly.

# Fish and Snails and Crabs and Whales

Miss Sparks said sadly, "Delaney,
will you tell me why you
do not want to do a presentation?"
Delaney said, "Oh, Miss Sparks!
I can't read as well as Skylar and Avery.
I can't draw as well as Hallie and Lindy.
I can't move as fast as
Connor and Gwen.
I can't be as funny as
Logan, Nathan, and Spencer."

Miss Sparks said, "I understand.

You have been comparing yourself

to other children

and it has made you sad."

"Yes!" said Delaney.

"Everyone does everything

better than I do."

Miss Sparks said, "I know something

that you do better than anyone else."

Delaney said, "You do?"

"Yes," said Miss Sparks.

"You are the best at being you."

Delaney smiled just a little bit.

Miss Sparks said,

"Every day you hum

and whistle and sing.

You love music.

And you love to share

your love of music."

Miss Sparks played a few

notes on the piano.

She said, "Remember

when we sang

this morning?

Our whole class was happy

because of you,

the one and only Delaney.

You are very good at

making people happy with music."

Miss Sparks gave Delaney a little hug.

Delaney thought about what

Miss Sparks had said.

Then Delaney smiled a big smile.

She jumped up and said,

"I think I have an idea

for a presentation."

"Splendid!" said Miss Sparks.

She was smiling too.

The sparkles on her eyeglasses

were glittering.

At last it was the day for

Miss Sparks's class to present its

program about sea creatures.

All the children were excited.

Students from other classes

came to Miss Sparks's classroom.

The visiting students sat on the floor.

First, Avery and Skylar told

interesting facts about whales.

The visiting students clapped.

Then, Hallie and Lindy showed

pretty drawings of seabirds.

The visiting students said, "Oooh!"

Next, Connor and Gwen walked

sideways very fast, like crabs.

The visiting students said, "Wow!"

After that, Logan, Nathan, and Spencer
told funny poems, riddles, and jokes.
The visiting students
laughed and laughed and laughed.
Finally, Miss Sparks sat at the piano.
She said, "Our last
presentation is by Delaney."
Delaney stood up.
She had a tambourine.

She said to the visiting students,

"My presentation is different because

everyone in our class is in it.

We are going to sing a song for you.

I wrote new words

to a song you all know."

Delaney began to play

the tambourine.

The other children pretended to row.

The children sang together,

"Row, row, row your boat.

Look and you will see.

Fish and snails and

crabs and whales,

swimming in the sea."

"Hurray!" the visiting

students cheered.

They clapped and clapped.

They loved Delaney's song!

Delaney said, "Now let's all sing

'Row, Row, Row Your Boat' together."

Everyone sang,

"Row, row, row your boat

gently down the stream."

Delaney smiled as she sang.

She was happy that the students had
liked her song about fish and
snails and crabs and whales.
She was even happier that
everyone was singing
"Row, Row, Row Your Boat"
together now.
But Delaney was happiest of
all that she was herself,
the one and only Delaney,
who made people
happy with music.
Delaney sang,
"Merrily, merrily,
merrily, merrily,
life is but a dream."

# Dear Parents . . .

Your child is a one-of-a-kind kid, with a style and a smile all her own. But she's at an age now when she's comparing herself to others more than ever before. Who's the fastest runner at school? Who's the best reader? Who's the funniest or the friendliest or the smartest? Like Delaney, your child is figuring out who she is by measuring herself against her peers, and she might fear she's coming up short.

Take advantage of the attention she's giving to others by showing her that it's our differences that make us interesting. Try the following activities, designed to encourage your child to appreciate those differences in others and in herself. You can help her identify her special talents and traits and remind her that she's already mastered one skill—the art of being her one and only self, the precious girl you love.

# All Sorts of Ways

Show your child that when it comes to people, nobody is "good," "better," or "best"—just "different." Celebrating those differences will help your child understand and appreciate the world around her, and she'll feel more pride in her own unique abilities, too.

• Ask your child to draw a picture of a familiar object, such as a tree or a house. Draw your own picture, and then compare yours to hers. Say something such as, "Look! We drew our trees differently. Mine has four branches and yours has three. Mine has a thick trunk and yours is skinnier. People have **all sorts of ways** of drawing and doing things. Wouldn't it be boring if we all did things exactly the same way?"

- Help your child and her friends make homemade instruments. Make drums out of empty oatmeal containers, maracas by filling cans with beads, and tambourines by tying jingle bells around paper plates. Then sing a familiar song and invite the "band" to play along. Talk about how **people are like instruments.** Say, "We all sound different and look different and do different things, but when we play together, we're like one big band. And we sound great!"

- Ask your child to pick out a family photo, and play the **Favorites** game. Can she tell you what each family member likes to do best? Is Mom's favorite thing planting flowers? Is Dad's favorite thing making Sunday morning breakfast? What are your child's favorite activities? Ask her what would happen if everyone in the family liked exactly the same things. What if everyone disliked all the same things?

- Plan activities that showcase the different ways family members do the same thing. Make a pizza dinner, and invite everyone to "personalize" slices with favorite ingredients. Then dance to the radio, and take turns showing off different **made-up moves!**

# One-of-a-Kind Kid

Your child relies on you and her peers to help her figure out what's most special about her. You can build her self-confidence while showing her how to look inward instead of outward for reassurance that she's one of a kind.

- Help your child discover the **ways she learns best.** Reread page 14 of *The One and Only Delaney,* and ask your child to imagine that she's a member of Miss Sparks's class. Which part of the sea creature presentation would your child want to help with? Does she like to share facts that she read in a book? Draw pictures of things she loves? Act like her favorite creature? Or sing a song she makes up herself? Respect her personal  style.

- Encourage your child to draw a **talent tree** on poster board. Identify her talents and talents-to-be by brainstorming all the activities she enjoys. Help her write the activities on paper leaves and tape them to the tree, putting those she does well at the top and those she wants to work on lower on the tree. As she gets better at those things, she can move them up the tree!

- Praise the traits underlying your child's talents. Reward her with a blue ribbon for **bravery** when she tries something new, or a new box of Band-aids for her **persistence** in getting back on her bike after a tumble. Praise her **enthusiasm,** too, when she has fun doing something that's still difficult. Say, "You sure seem to have fun when you dance. I like to see that smile!"

- Discourage "being the best" thinking. Take your child to sporting events, plays, or concerts to show her that there's **room in this world** for *many* talented people. Ask her what she admires most about the performers, and what she admires most about herself, too. Then stand your child in front of the mirror and say, "There are many athletes [or artists or musicians] in this world, but there's only one *you*."

# The Gifts She Shares

As your child explores her special qualities, remind her that her best "gifts" are those that she can share with others. She can make friends and family happy by inviting them to enjoy something she loves, and when they return the favor, she might learn something new, too!

• Show your child the value of her talents by asking her to **teach you something** you don't know how to do, such as play a computer game or sing a song that she learned at school. Remind her that it's difficult to do something for the first time, so she'll need to be patient with you. Say, "It's hard to remember all those words, but maybe if we sing it again, I'll learn them." When you've got it down, thank her for sharing her time and her talents with you.

- At holidays and birthdays, encourage your child to give **gifts from the heart,** such as a dance she performs in her ballet costume, a painting in a special frame, or a coupon for time that she'll spend with someone. Family members will receive a priceless gift, and your child will receive something, too—a boost of confidence in herself and her abilities.

- Sharing gifts is a **two-way street.** Are there skills your child wants to learn? Help her list or draw those things, and ask her if she knows anyone who enjoys doing them. Can her sister teach her a few karate kicks? Can a classmate help her learn to count to ten in Spanish? Role-play ways that she can ask these people for their help and ways that she can thank them afterward, perhaps by sharing a talent of her own.

- Send your child off to Show-and-Tell **armed with a new way** of doing or learning something. Does she write letters to Grandma using new spelling words? Did she memorize the parts of a plant by pretending to be one, growing up from the ground? Classmates might benefit from seeing or hearing about those ways of learning—or have clever ideas of their own!

This story and the "Dear Parents" activities were developed with guidance from the Hopscotch Hill School advisory board.

Dominic Gullo is a professor of Early Childhood Education at Queens College, City University of New York. He is a member of the governing board of the National Association for the Education of Young Children, and he is a consultant to school districts across the country in the areas of early childhood education, curriculum, and assessment.

Margaret Jensen has taught beginning reading for 32 years and is currently a math resource teacher in the Madison Metropolitan School District, Wisconsin. She has served on committees for the International Reading Association and the Wisconsin State Reading Association, and has been president of the Madison Area Reading Council. She has presented at workshops and conferences in the areas of reading, writing, and children's literature.

Kim Miller is a school psychologist at Stephens Elementary in Madison, Wisconsin, where she works with children, parents, and teachers to help solve—and prevent—problems related to learning and adjustment to the classroom setting.

Virginia Pickerell has worked with teachers and parents as an educational consultant and counselor within the Madison Metropolitan School District. She has researched and presented workshops on topics such as learning processes, problem solving, and creativity. She is also a former director of Head Start.